The Newest Princess

by Melody Mews illustrated by Ellen Stubbings

LITTLE SIMON

New York   London   Toronto   Sydney   New Delhi

LITTLE SIMON

An imprint of Simon & Schuster Children's Publishing Division
1230 Avenue of the Americas, New York, New York 10020
First Little Simon hardcover edition February 2020. Copyright © 2020 by Simon & Schuster, Inc.
All rights reserved, including the right of reproduction in whole or in part in any form.
LITTLE SIMON is a registered trademark of Simon & Schuster, Inc., and associated colophon is a trademark of Simon & Schuster, Inc. For information about special discounts for bulk purchases, please contact Simon & Schuster Special Sales at 1-866-506-1949
or business@simonandschuster.com.
The Simon & Schuster Speakers Bureau can bring authors to your live event.
For more information or to book an event contact the Simon & Schuster Speakers Bureau
at 1-866-248-3049 or visit our website at www.simonspeakers.com.
Designed by Laura Roode. The text of this book was set in Banda.
Manufactured in the United States of America 0520 BVG 10 9 8 7 6 5 4 3 2
Library of Congress Cataloging-in-Publication Data
Names: Mews, Melody, author. | Stubbings, Ellen, illustrator.
Title: The newest princess / by Melody Mews ; illustrated by Ellen Stubbings. Description: First Little Simon paperback edition. | New York : Little Simon, 2020. | Series: Itty Bitty Princess Kitty ; #1 | Summary: Itty is excited to learn that she will soon be a princess, until she begins to worry about all the changes her new role brings. Identifiers: LCCN 2019022085 (print) | LCCN 2019022410 (eBook) | ISBN 9781534454934 (pbk : alk. paper) | ISBN 9781534454941 (hc : alk. paper) | ISBN 9781534454958 (eBook) Subjects: CYAC: Cats—Fiction. | Animals—Infancy—Fiction. | Princesses—Fiction. | Change—Fiction. | Unicorns—Fiction. | Fantasy.
Classification: LCC PZ7.1.M4976 New 2019 (print) | LCC PZ7.1.M4976 (eBook) | DDC [E]—dc23
LC record available at https://lccn.loc.gov/2019022085
LC eBook record available at https://lccn.loc.gov/2019022410

Contents

The Fairy's Announcement

It was a beautiful, sunny afternoon in Lollyland. Itty Bitty Kitty and her best friend, Luna Unicorn, were playing in the field of flowers behind Itty's home, the royal palace of Lollyland.

"I spy with my little eye . . . a

fairy!" Luna exclaimed.

"A fairy?" Itty giggled. "Good one, Luna! We are more than a hop, skip, and a jump from Fairy Forest. There are no fairies in this field!"

"She's right, Itty!"

Itty turned to the sparkling flower that had just spoken.

"Really?" Now Itty believed it. Flowers rarely spoke. When they did, it was because they had something very important to say.

Itty looked up and saw a tiny fairy flying toward them. A moment later, the fairy landed on a flower. She was no larger than a butterfly. From the miniature trumpet she carried, Itty knew exactly what kind of fairy she was.

"That's an announcement fairy!" Luna cried.

"Maybe she's looking for the palace," Itty whispered. She moved

closer to the fairy. "Are you looking for my parents, the King and Queen?"

"No, Itty Bitty Kitty, this announcement is for *you!*" the fairy squeaked.

Suddenly the field became so quiet you could hear the water of Starfish Falls rushing in the distance.

The little fairy blew her tiny trumpet. Three jingling notes rang out. "Itty Bitty Kitty, I have been sent by the shooting stars with some *fairy* exciting news!" The fairy paused for one dramatic moment before continuing. "In one week, your eighth shooting star will arrive!"

Itty was speechless. Luna was speechless.

The fairy threw her teeny hands up. "Don't you know what that means?" she squeaked, tapping her foot impatiently.

Of course Itty knew what it meant. So did Luna, and everyone else in Lollyland. In just one week, Itty was going to become a princess. She would no longer be Itty Bitty Kitty. She would be . . . Itty Bitty Princess Kitty!

♥ chapter 2 ♥

Princess-to-Be!

Itty and Luna thanked the fairy and then raced to the palace. As they ran, a cloud of glitter followed them. When Luna got excited, her horn sprayed glitter!

"I can't wait to tell my parents!" Itty exclaimed as they reached

the front door of the palace.

"This is SO EXCITING!" Luna squealed.

"Um, Luna, can you maybe *not* do that inside?" Itty asked as a poof of glitter shot into the air.

"Right." Luna nodded. She closed her eyes and concentrated. When she opened them, she giggled and a little bit of glitter landed on Itty's nose.

"Good enough," Itty said, grabbing her best friend's hand and running inside.

"Mom? Dad? Where are youuuu?" Itty called. "Hey, what time is it?" she asked when no one responded.

"Let's see," said Luna, "the last time the mermaids sang, it was eleven notes, so it's just after eleven."

"Just after eleven . . . ," Itty said, thinking. "They must be in the climbing room! Follow me!"

Sure enough, that's just where the King and Queen of Lollyland

were. Queen Kitty was perched high atop her favorite climbing structure. She watched as King Kitty leaped from one perch to another.

"Mom! Dad! Did you hear the news?" Itty called.

Queen Kitty wiggled her ears. "What did you lose?"

"No, I said . . . DID YOU HEAR—"

"There's no need to shout, darling," Itty's mom replied, gracefully leaping to the ground.

Itty's dad landed a few moments later with a less graceful thump.

"I   SAID"—Itty   lowered   her voice—"I said, did you hear the news? An   announcement   fairy told us . . . she told us . . ."

"Itty's eighth shooting star is coming next week!" Luna exclaimed.

Queen Kitty nodded. "Our announcement fairy came last week," she explained. "It was hard to keep the surprise from you, Itty. But now that you know, the fun can begin!"

"The fun?" Itty repeated, her
big eyes growing even wider.

"Yes!" King Kitty cried. "Tonight,
we begin our preparations!"

Gumdrop
Daydreams

"Sorry my room is so messy," Itty said to Luna a few minutes later. "My mom asked me to clean it, but I forgot."

"That's okay." Luna smiled. "I'm pretty used to it by now. Even your unmade bed doesn't bother me anymore."

Itty laughed. It was true: As a kitty, she loved snuggling in rumpled blankets. She swatted a toy mouse off a nearby beanbag chair so Luna could sit down. She knew it was Luna's favorite spot.

The magic beans inside were super squishy!

"I wonder if you will still have to clean your room once you are a princess," Luna said as she sank into the soft chair.

"Ooh, I hope not!" Itty said as she settled on her bed. "I wonder if I'll get some fancy princess dresses."

"Yes!" Luna cheered. "What kind would you like?"

"Well . . ." Itty had never thought about it before. She'd always worn regular kitty clothes. But surely being a *princess* kitty meant having special princess clothes!

"Nothing too lacy, because my claws might get stuck," Itty said. "And nothing too stiff, because

I like to run and jump. Maybe velvet?"

"Velvet is soooo fancy!" Luna agreed. "What else?"

"Soft silk dresses," Itty purred. "As silky as flower petals."

"Maybe the dress can smell like flowers too!" Luna exclaimed.

"I want a dress that smells like kitty treats!" Itty cried. "Or one with kitty treat buttons, so I can snack on them if I get hungry!"

"What about a cotton candy dress?" Luna squealed.

"Or a gumdrop dress!"

The girls burst into giggles as they both said this at the same time. Moments later they heard the song of the Lollyland mermaids. They sang twelve notes, which meant it was twelve o'clock. It also meant Itty and Luna were late. They were supposed to meet their friends Esme and Chipper at the Goodie Grove.

Meet Esme and Chipper

"If we catch a cloud, we won't be *too* late," Itty said, running to the window. A cloud was there waiting, so Itty and Luna hopped aboard.

"To the Goodie Grove!" Itty cried, and off they zoomed. They flew over Starfish Falls and took

a shortcut through Fairy Forest
before landing in the center of
the Goodie Grove.

This was where all the food in
Lollyland came from. Fruits and
vegetables grew there, but so

did lollipops, cupcakes, and more. There were bushes of cotton candy and streams of syrup. There were even trees that could make a whole meal for you. You just had to tell your order to a waiter bird,

who would fly it up to the tippy-
top to be made on the spot.

Esme Butterfly and Chipper
Bunny were already there.

"Hello, Luna and Itty Bitty

Princess Kitty!" Esme squealed as she and Chipper rushed over.

"You know already?" Itty couldn't believe how fast the news had traveled.

"Yes, all of Lollyland knows!" Chipper cried. "You know how chatty fairies can be."

"Ahem!" squeaked a syrup fairy who was collecting syrup from a nearby stream. Placing her bucket down, she put her tiny hands on her hips.

"Oh, my friend meant that as a compliment," Itty assured the fairy, who shrugged and went back to work.

"So, what should we play?" Itty asked her friends. "Capture the Daisy? Cat, Cat, Mouse? Hide and Seek in the lollipop garden?"

"Itty," Esme said, suddenly looking concerned, "can you still play with us once you're a princess?"

"Yeah, won't you be too busy doing princess stuff?" Chipper fretted.

"What? No way!" Itty said firmly.

"Good! We were worried about that," Esme said. She looked relieved. "And can you still camp by Starfish Falls? And have ice cream sundae parties on Saturdays?"

"Of course!" Itty replied. But a tiny doubt was starting to creep into her mind. Were things going to change once she was a princess?

♥ chapter 5 ♥

Some Royal Changes

A delicious smell from the kitchen told Itty it was dinnertime even before the Lollyland mermaids sang six notes.

When Itty arrived at the dining room, Queen Kitty explained that they were having Itty's favorite

meal to celebrate. "Let's eat and then we'll talk about the special preparations."

Itty looked down. It wasn't just her favorite meal—it was all her favorite foods: spaghetti with pink sauce, raspberry jam sandwiches, mashed marshmallows, candied beets, and there was even a

twenty-six-layer confetti cake!

Itty ate as much as she could. "Thank you!" she said to her parents when she was totally stuffed. "So what are the special preparations?" she asked. She was eager to hear what her parents meant.

"Well, darling, some things

will happen before you become Lollyland's princess," said the Queen. "For starters, the royal groomer will come tomorrow to create your princess hairstyle."

"My princess hairstyle?" Itty asked.

"The royal architect will be coming to plan your new bedroom," the King added.

"My new bedroom?" Itty repeated.

"And you will meet the royal tutor, of course," her mom continued.

"The royal tutor?" Itty said. "Why do I need a tutor?"

"You will be palace-schooled once you become princess," the Queen replied. "You'll no longer go to school."

Itty gulped. These "special preparations" sounded like a whole lot of changes.

"That's enough for now," the Queen said gently. "We know it's a lot to take in. Why don't

you go rest up for your big day tomorrow?"

Itty kissed her parents good night and headed up to her bedroom. She searched and searched for a comfy spot on her bed and couldn't seem to find one.

Finally, she curled up in a little ball in her favorite spot. But it was a while before she fell asleep.

Too New

The royal groomer, a French poodle, had already tried three hairstyles on Itty, but she didn't like any of them.

The first one was too fluffy.

"I look like a cotton candy bush," Itty said.

The second one was too spikey.

"Ouch," Itty said after touching her hairdo.

And the third one was too long. Itty couldn't walk without tripping over her hair!

"We will try again later," the royal groomer said after fixing Itty's hair back to her usual style. Itty could tell the groomer was disappointed.

Next it was time for Itty to meet with the royal tutor, a very wise-looking cat.

The first lesson was about fractions of apple pies.

Itty scratched her head. "We just count apples at my school.

We haven't gotten to pies yet."

The next lesson was about telling time.

"I just listen for the mermaids to sing and then I count the notes." Itty shrugged.

But when it came time for the lesson about Lollyland geography, it was finally Itty's time to shine. She knew things about Lollyland that even her tutor didn't know!

"I go camping at Starfish Falls," Itty explained. "That's how I know about the Rock Candy Rocks and the secret passageway to the Crystal Caves."

When the tutor left that evening, Itty was feeling overwhelmed. She headed up to her room. Maybe it would make her feel better to be in her own little space. But when she got to her room, the royal architect was there with a crew of builder fairies.

"Can you come back later?" the royal architect asked when she saw Itty.

Itty nodded and quickly turned away. She didn't want anyone to see the tears in her eyes.

Choosing a Tiara

The next day Itty woke up with a funny feeling in her tummy. When she opened her eyes and saw the big hole in her wall, everything that had happened over the past few days came rushing back. The princess hairstyles she didn't like, the lessons with the tutor she didn't understand, the construction in her room . . .

She was about to become a princess, but she couldn't have felt less like herself.

Itty's mom scratched at her door, asking her to come downstairs to meet with the royal jeweler. Itty sighed, wondering what kinds of changes this meeting would bring.

But to Itty's delight, the royal jeweler, an elegant cat sparkling with jewels, was there to help her choose her princess tiara.

The royal jeweler
had a display
case filled with
beautiful tiaras.
And Itty was allowed
to try on every
single one! One tiara was made
of sparkling blue sapphires the
size of Itty's paws. Another tiara,
this one made of
shiny gold, had cat
faces engraved on
it. And yet another
glittered so much
that Itty thought it

was covered in
fairy dust.

"It *is* covered
in fairy dust!" the
royal jeweler exclaimed.

But one tiara, located on the
tippy-top shelf of the case, caught
Itty's eye. She pointed to it and
the jeweler reached for it. It was

made of smooth, gleaming gold, and at its center was a pink, heart-shaped gemstone. The moment it touched her head, Itty knew it was the tiara for her.

"I think you found the perfect one," the jeweler said.

"I agree." The Queen nodded, proud tears shining in her eyes.

Itty looked at her reflection in the mirror. The tiara was the most beautiful thing she had ever seen. She definitely looked like a princess. But she sure didn't feel like one.

chapter 8

Itty Bitty NOT-So-Princess Kitty

The next day at school, Itty told Luna about all the things that were going to be changing. Luna was so excited for Itty that glitter rained down.

"I think I would have chosen the ruby tiara!" Luna squealed.

"No, maybe the fairy dust one! Did they have any with emeralds? Or onyx? Onyx matches your eyes."

Noticing that her friend wasn't smiling, Luna paused. "I'm sorry,

Itty!" Luna said quickly. "What do I know about tiaras? I bet you picked the perfect one. The absolute prettiest one, for sure. I—"

"It's not that, Luna," Itty said quietly. "I love my tiara. It's pretty much the only good thing that's happened since I got the news about my shooting star."

"What?!" Luna exclaimed. "Itty, what do you mean? All these new things sound so amazing! So spectacular! So . . . princess-y!"

"That's just it." Itty sighed. "These things don't make me feel more like a princess. They just make me feel less like myself. I don't want a different hairstyle or a new room. I don't want to be palace-schooled. I like coming to school *here*."

Itty looked around. She was going to miss playing on the rainbow slide at recess with Luna. She was going to miss sitting in a circle with her friends during story time. She was going to miss her desk, with her sharp pencils and pink erasers that smelled like ice cream.

Most of all, Itty was going to miss seeing her friends. She felt a little scared, and a little confused. And she felt something else. She felt that perhaps she wasn't meant to be a princess after all.

Be Your Own Princess

That evening there was a scratch at Itty's bedroom door. She was surprised to see both of her parents standing there. They walked into her room and hopped onto her bed.

"Come sit and talk with us,"

her mom said, patting the space between them.

Itty knew what her parents were going to say. They were going to tell her that a mistake had been made, that she was not meant to be a princess. She sat down between her parents, tucking her paws up underneath her body, and waited.

"Sweetheart, we want to talk to you about the preparations," her dad began. "Do you *want* to get a new royal hairstyle? Or a new room?"

Itty felt tears forming in her

eyes. "No," she admitted.

"Do you want to be palace-schooled?" her mom asked.

"No," Itty whispered. She didn't want to disappoint her parents, but she had to be honest.

"I'm not good at this!" she cried. "I don't want a new hairstyle, or a royal tutor, or a new room! None of those things feel like . . . me." Itty took a deep breath. "And I like being me. I guess I'm not supposed to be a princess after all. That's what you are here to tell me, right?"

"Oh, Itty . . ." The King and Queen pulled Itty into a hug.

"That's not what we were going to say," the Queen replied, kissing Itty's head. "We were going to tell you that you don't have to do any of those things if you don't want to."

"What?" Itty almost couldn't believe her ears.

"Those preparations are meant to make a young kitty feel royal," the King explained. "All the past princes and princesses wanted those special measures, but they are not required. And you *are* the princess. The shooting star says so. You can be the princess you want to be!"

"I can be the princess I want to be," Itty repeated. As she said it, she felt it in her heart.

The Shooting Star

The big day had finally arrived!

Itty felt like she was floating on a cloud. At school, the teacher dismissed class early so everyone could get home before the shooting star celebrations began.

When Itty got home, she

gasped. Gold streamers dangled from the ceilings and glitter-filled bubbles floated all around.

Itty's parents were there to greet her.

"We have a surprise for you, princess-to-be," the King said, taking Itty by the paw. He led her upstairs, stopping just before her bedroom door.

"I know you said you didn't want a new room," he began. "But your mother and I thought you might want to see what the royal architect did, and then decide."

Itty took a deep breath and opened the door.

First she noticed the things that were still the same, like her bed with rumpled blankets and the squishy beanbag chair filled with magic beans.

Then she noticed all the new things, like the giant climbing structure with fluffy pillows at the tippy-top, and a huge bookshelf filled with brand-new books. She saw the treats dispenser and felt her tummy rumble just from looking at it. And her bed wasn't the same bed after all! It still had the same crumpled covers

she loved, but it was a new bed
with a beautiful canopy on top.
The closet was three times the
size of Itty's old closet, and it was
filled with princess dresses! And

Itty noticed not one of them was made of lace. She thought about what Luna would say. She'd love Itty's new room. And Itty had to admit . . . *she* loved it too.

Itty grinned and turned to her dad. "I guess I can accept one new thing!"

"I thought you might say that," her dad purred, pulling her in for a hug. "And this," he said as he pointed to a beautiful glass case, "is for your shooting star when it arrives."

"Speaking of your shooting star," said the Queen, "it's time."

Itty went to the balcony with her mom and dad. A few moments later, a brilliant light flew across the sky. Itty's shooting star was the most spectacular sight Lollyland had ever seen. Itty was so starstruck, she couldn't even hear the other creatures cheering, or the mermaids singing, or the fairies clapping. The star came closer and closer. Finally, it arrived. It floated for a moment right in front of Itty's nose.

"Take it, darling," said Itty's mom. And Itty did. As she grabbed it, she felt her heart swell, and she knew in that moment that she really was meant to be a princess. She was still herself, but she was now Itty Bitty Princess Kitty.

Here's a sneak
peek at Itty's next
royal adventure!

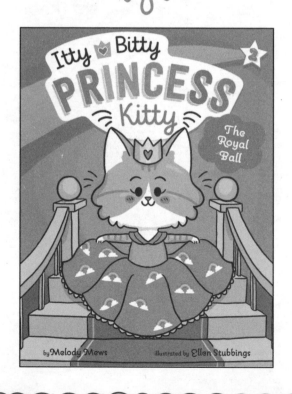

Knock-knock.

"Are you awake, Itty?"

Itty Bitty Princess Kitty yawned. "Yes, Mom," she murmured sleepily.

"Don't fall back asleep in that cozy new bed of yours," the Queen called from outside her room.

Itty giggled. Her new bed was part of a whole new bedroom that was fit for a princess. Just yesterday she had simply been Itty Bitty Kitty. But then her eighth shooting star had arrived, which meant that today—and forever— she was Itty Bitty Princess Kitty, Princess of Lollyland!

Itty got out of bed and walked toward her new closet. She paused in front of the display case that held her glowing shooting star.

Itty couldn't believe how beautiful it was.

And she still couldn't believe she was a princess. Some of the changes, like her new room, had excited Itty. But others, like getting a new hairdo or being palace-schooled, hadn't. Those changes had made Itty worry she wouldn't feel like herself anymore. Luckily, her parents, the King and Queen of Lollyland, had explained that she could be the princess she wanted to be. She didn't have to change her hair or be palace-schooled.

I'm glad I still go to school with my friends, Itty thought.

For more books, activities, and adorable adventures
visit IntheMiddleBooks.com.